Alphabet Kingdom

by Lauren A. Parent and mo mcgee

albatross apple snails armadillo giant anteater aardwolf aye
bandicool badger bobcat bushbaby bowerbird burmese cat bla
civet camel cavy chipmunk cormorant cobra cougar dingo do
dholes duck painted dog tasmanian devil elephant emu echi
emerald snake emperor penguin egret flamingo fennec fox
feral cat flying fish finch gorilla gecko guenon monkey gira
hamsters hornbill rock hyrax howler monkey honeybee he
iguana impala indri ibis jacana jaguar japanese dormouse
japanese macaque kudu kingsnake kinkajou kiwi ka
komodo dragon kudu king lizard llama lion lemu
manatee mongoose moon rat motm bobak marmot mandr
n-tailed macaque brazza monkey mission blue butterfly n
nene goose nutha night snake numbat norway lemming
opossum owl oc otter os penguin porcupine parr
giant panda peacock praying mantas eastern c
cottontail quail quetzal rabbit red panda racco
sloth snake sea lion tree shrew squirrel skinner siam
blue tit toad tree kangaroo tabby treefrog eurasian treecre
beralla vulture vista vesper verio rock wallaby walrus
wild boar wildcat wagtail western grebe woodmouse
woodmouse yellowtail yellow-eyed cuckooshrike zel

FULCRUM

GOLDEN, COLORADO

Allison the annoyed aardvark arranges assorted appointments for Alex the anxious anteater.

Barry the bear borrows
bunches of bananas from his best buddy,

Billy the buffalo,
behind the ballpark.

Christina
the crafty
crocodile
creates
classy
coats

for confident caracals
on the catwalk.

Douglas the dapper duck doodles delicate donuts for Danny the delighted painted dog.

Emily the elegant elephant eagerly elopes

with Ernie the earnest egret.

Freddie the frazzled flying fish
frantically flees from a fire truck
while fidgeting with five
frilly frames.

G abby the gracious giraffe
gainfully gathers gorillas at her
glamorous gazebo and greets

Georgia the
gentle great ape.

Hilarious
hungry hamsters
hastily hassle
Henry the
happy hippo.

Izzy the intelligent iguana is isolated in her igloo imagining ice blocking with Ian the insane ibis.

Jacob the jovial jaguar
jauntily juggles jackrabbits

for Jerry the jackal
and Joseph the joey.

Kenneth the klutzy
kingfisher keenly avoids

kamikaze kites kicked by
Kristy the kooky kangaroo.

Luciano the laughing langur
loves his laptop and his lavish
life with Lacy the
lounging lizard.

Monty the mangy
mongoose mockingly

moves Manty the manatee's
many marbles.

Nicki the nippy nightingale noisily nags Nancy the nimble nene goose.

Ophelia the oryx observes Olivia the obsessive ostrich objecting to Orville the obnoxious otter.

Patty the pesky parrot persistently pesters Patrick the plump penguin.

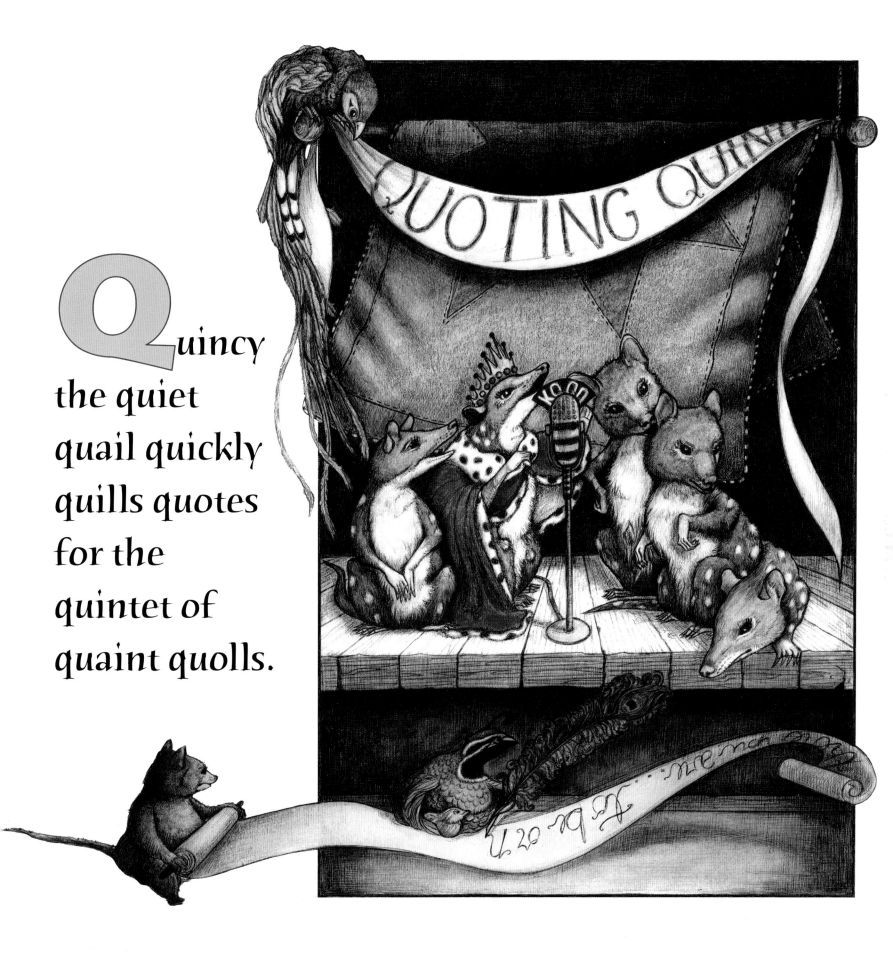

Quincy the quiet quail quickly quills quotes for the quintet of quaint quolls.

Rachael the rascally raccoon

rapidly robs Robert the rich rabbit.

Stacey the sneaky snake serpentines

subtly toward Steven the
unsuspecting spider monkey.

T

iffany the
tame tiger thoughtfully thanks

Thomas the   taciturn turtle
for the   terrific telephone.

Ulysses the urbane uakari monkey uncovers a ukulele under ugly umbrellas with Uma the unexcited ural owl.

Various vermin vigorously vanish from Virgil the vibrant vulture's views of the vast valley.

Willard the wallaby

whimsically wanders through waterfalls

wondering where
Wally the whistling walrus went.

Xavier the exotic X-ray fish yodels for **Y**onnie the yawning yellowtail, while **Z**uZu the zealous zebu zanily zips on her zeppelin.

Library of Congress Cataloging-in-Publication Data

Parent, Lauren A.
  Alphabet kingdom / by Lauren A. Parent & Mo
McGee.
      p. cm.
  Summary: Animals ranging from Allison the annoyed
aardvark to ZuZu the zealous zebu introduce the letters
of the alphabet through adventure, wordplay, and
elaborate illustrations.
  ISBN-13: 978-1-55591-643-5 (pbk.)
  ISBN-10: 1-55591-643-0 (pbk.)
  [1. Animals--Fiction. 2. Alphabet.] I. McGee, Mo. II.
Title.
  PZ7.P2163Alp 2009
  [E]--dc22
                                        2009012032

Printed in China by P. Chan & Edward
0 9 8 7 6 5 4 3 2 1

Design by Ann W. Douden

Fulcrum Publishing
4690 Table Mountain Drive, Suite 100
Golden, Colorado 80403
800-992-2908 • 303-277-1623
www.fulcrumbooks.com

Unique unicorns